BOBS AND Tweets

Trick or Tweet

by PEPPER SPRINGFIELD

illustrated by KRISTY CALDWELL

SCHOLASTIC INC.

For Rebecca and John
–PS
For my resident storyteller.
–KC

ISBN 978-1-338-36100-1

10 9 8 7 6 5 4 3 2 1   18 19 20 21 22

Printed in the U.S.A.   40
First edition, September 2018

Book design: Becky James
Flatter: Jess Worby

TABLE OF CONTENTS

CHAPTER 1
ZOMBIES

Dean Bob sets his crown on top of his head.

He looks in the mirror, then kneels by his bed.

He calls to his dog, "Chopper. Come. Sit.

I want to adjust your mer-tail a bit."

Dean takes his trident and goes to the door.

He hears lots of noise coming from the first floor.

"Dean! Chopper! Come down! We are all set!

Slime showers! Ghost Light Shows! Bobs' best funhouse yet."

Six zombies are waiting on the front porch.
Each zombie is holding a pumpkin-head torch.
"Say cheese!" Bob Four cries. "Strike a pose. Look at me.
We need a good photo of our family."

"I have to get going. Bye now," says Dean.
Your funhouse looks ready for a Bobs' Halloween."
"Let's all go," whoop the Bobs, "it will be fun."
"No thanks," says Dean, "you will scare everyone."

CHAPTER 2
STRING BEANS

King Neptune and Mer-dog cross Bonefish Street
They hurry to pick up Dean's best friend, Lou Tweet.
Six Tweets dressed as string beans come to the door.
Lou's stuff is spread out all over the floor.

"Lou," peep six Tweets, "Dean and Chopper are here."
"Tweets!" complains Lou. "We do not need this gear.
Walkie-talkies? A compass? A hiker's headlamp?
Do you think we are going to survival camp?"

"Remember our deal," the Tweets peep to Lou.
"Safety First! Or we come trick-or-treating with you."
"Safety first," Dean agrees, "Tweet rules are clear.
You can trust us alone with no grown-ups this year."

"We made this cool map of each house on our street.
We check off each box and write down each treat.
When our map is complete, we will send it in.
If ours is the best block in town, then we win."

"Look Tweets," adds Lou, "Dean's Bobs went to the mall.
To get these huge bags for our Halloween haul."

As they are leaving, two ghosts and one hawk
shout "trick or treat," then dash up the Tweets' walk.
"Hey kiddos," says Lou, "there is no need to rush.
You get no candy here. Just a light-up toothbrush."

CHAPTER 3

CANDY FISH

Lifeguard Mark's house is next, at the top of their map.
Mark answers the door in an orange swim cap.
"Come in trick-or-treaters, your costumes are cool.
Have we met? Do you guys come to the pool?"

"Mark," Lou Tweet cries, "it is Dean, and me, Lou!"
(Mark says with a wink "Oh yes. I know you.")
"My Tweets dress as veggies on Halloween.
This year they are string beans—healthy and green."

"Too boring for me! So I took tape and wire.
I made myself into a String Bean Vampire."
"I love it," says Mark, "you did such a good job.
What is your costume? Who are you Dean Bob?"

"My Bobs like to dress up as zombies from Mars.
Their costumes are bloody and covered with scars.
But I chose to be Neptune, King of the Sea.
It feels like a better costume for me."

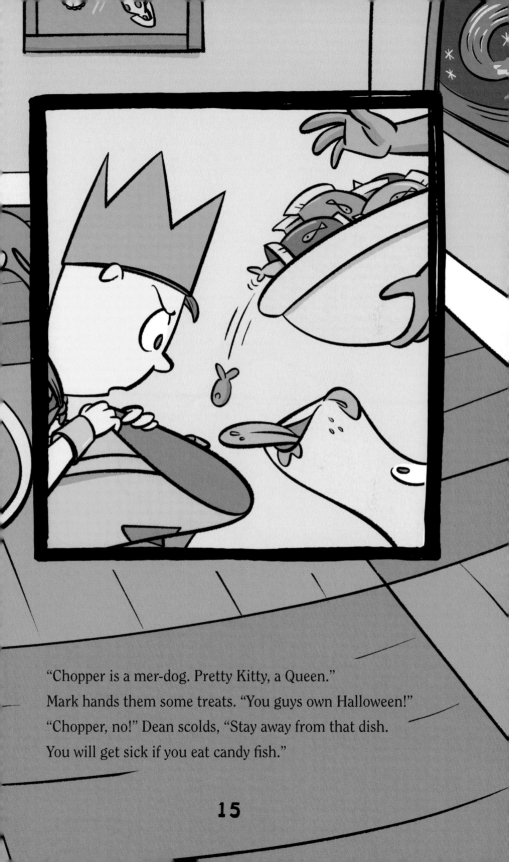

"Chopper is a mer-dog. Pretty Kitty, a Queen."
Mark hands them some treats. "You guys own Halloween!"
"Chopper, no!" Dean scolds, "Stay away from that dish.
You will get sick if you eat candy fish."

Dean pulls out a pen and takes off the cap.

He checks off Mark's house on their Halloween map.

Lou takes the pen, she writes neatly and slow.

Candy Fish from Mark; ten houses to go.

DEAN & LOU'S
HALLOWEEN BLOCK
"BONEFISH STREET"
WEETS
TOOTH
USHES
20
18
19
BOBS
SLIME
BALLS
17
CANDY
FISH FROM
MARK

CHAPTER 4
TRICK-OR-TREATING

They follow their map to one house then another.

They get baseball cookies from Chucky P's mother.

Sheriff Mo says her coins are each worth thirteen cents.

Ms. Pat and her pets are US Presidents.

The O'Learys give goldfish; the Lees hand out gummies.
Mr. Bigtree shares bags of marshmallow mummies.
Dean checks off each house. Lou records every treat.
While Chopper keeps looking for something to eat.

"Those triplets," Dean points, "are dressed up as rats."
"Uh oh," says Lou, "those kids look like brats."
Just then, sure enough, one rat does a flip.
And lands on the Queen's tail, right at the tip.

Pretty Kitty is mad! She leaps in the air.

She hisses—claws out—which gives Chopper a scare.

Dean's dog and Lou's cat take off in a run

These. Pets. Are. Having. No. Halloween. Fun.

CHAPTER 5
THE SCARIEST HOUSE

"Where are they," Lou whispers. "This yard is SO dark.

"Wait, listen!" says Dean, "I just heard Chopper bark."

Lou shines her headlamp "Look! Over there!

By the door, under that red rocking chair."

Dean and Lou creep carefully, low to the ground.
They try really hard to not make a sound.
The door opens a crack. Lou sees a boy's face.
"Oh phew, it's the new kid. Sal, is this your place?"

"Hey guys," say Sal, "we just moved in here.
We are not doing much Halloween stuff this year.
My mom has to work. Gramps is staying with me.
We are going to have pizza, then watch some TV."

"That's not fair, Sal" says Lou. "Not fair," echoes Dean.
"Come out with us Sal. You can't miss Halloween."
"I have nothing," Sal says, "no costume to wear."
"No problem-o," says Lou, "we three will share."

In just a few minutes, they get Sal dressed.
In Lou's string bean gloves and Gramp's old fishing vest.
Dean drapes a fishnet over Sal's head.
"Meet Sal, the Swamp Monster who sea creatures dread."

CHAPTER 6
BLACK OUT

Dean shows Sal the map, and Lou fills him in.

"We found a cool contest we know we can win.

We finished ten houses. We are working so hard.

We were close when our pets took off to your yard."

"The prizes are really awesome," adds Dean.

"We can win free costumes for next Halloween.

Plus five hundred dollars for a cause that does good.

And helps folks in need in our neighborhood."

As Dean is talking, they see a bright spark.
Then they hear a loud BOOM and the street lamps go dark.
A car alarms wails. Sal freezes with fright.
"A blackout!" says Lou, "on Halloween night."

Three friends and two pets stand in the pitch black.
"What now, guys?" frets Sal. "Should we head back?"
"No quitting!" says Dean, "with three houses to go.
We can see by Lou's headlamp. Let's go nice and slow."

"Safety First!" Lou reminds them, "we follow Tweet rules.
Remember we have all those survival tools."
Lou hands Dean the compass. He points it due North.
Dean shouts, "Follow King Neptune. Let us go forth."

They start walking. Sal cries, "Guys! Wait! Check your back!
I see zombies from Mars. It looks like an attack.
And there! On that side. Those shadows look mean."
"STOP, DROP, AND ROLL. We surrender," cries Dean.

CHAPTER 7
RESCUE

Lou picks up her head when she hears her Tweets say,
"Dean, Lou, Pretty Kitty—are you OK?"
Dean and Chopper stand up as six zombie Bobs moan.
"We were worried you were out in the dark on your own."

"A blackout!" says Dean, "did you hear any news?"
"Those Bobs!" the Tweets peep, "their funhouse blew a fuse."
"No way," cry the Bobs, "it was your Tweet creation.
Your glow-in-the-dark toothbrush charging station."

"Bobs!" the Tweets scold, "your disgusting slime shower uses too much electrical power."
"Tweets!" the Bobs yell, "this is the wrong day to wage a big war against tooth decay."

"STOP IT!" Lou yells, "You ruined our night.
We followed your rules. All you do is fight."

"We came out to save you," the Tweets peep to Lou.
"That's right!" The Bobs whoop: "zombies to the rescue."

"We did NOT need saving. We are fine." exclaims Lou.
"Now we can't finish our map thanks to you."
"We will not win the contest. We blew it." says Dean.
And you spoiled Sal's first Bonefish Street Halloween."

Six Tweets and six Bobs do not know what to say.
"You are right," the Tweets peep, "we got in your way."
"Come on," the Bobs whoop, "it is never too late.
To prove Bobs and Tweets can cooperate."

They chant: "Finish Your Map. Get Back on Track.
String beans and zombies: We all have your back!"

CHAPTER 8
FINISH. OUR. MAP.

Six zombies with torches light up the block.
Bob Six carries Chopper. He is too sick to walk.
With Lou on his left and Dean on his right
Sal rolls up the map and holds it real tight.

At Samir's they get popcorn. They go next, to Zach's.

Zach's mom gives them bookmarks tied up in cute packs.

At the third house, a basket sits out on a shelf.

Note: *Eddie is working. Please help yourself.*

"We did it!" cries Lou. "At last! We are done!
Let's go celebrate at Bobs' House of Fun."

"Too bad," Dean says. "Our house has no light.
Bobs' dancing ghost light show cannot work tonight."
"We got this," Tweets peep, "let's go make some power.
Tweets will light up Bobs' funhouse within half an hour."

So the Tweets ride ahead. The Bobs walk behind.
"Can we pick up my Gramps?" Sal asks, "Do you guys mind?
He is home all alone with nothing to do."
"We can stop on the way. No problem-o," says Lou.

CHAPTER 9
BOBS (AND TWEETS) HALLOWEEN FUNHOUSE

The funhouse is awesome, run on Tweet power.

Bob Four spends a long time in the slime shower.

Captain Jo'leen keeps the street closed to cars.

Mo and the Ruckers hand out sheriff stars.

Lawn monsters sway to the light show's rap beat.
Bonefish Streeters line up to get burgers to eat.
They dunk for apples. Take photos. Get showered with slime.
Everyone at this party has a great time.

At the game booth, Lifeguard Mark plays to win.

Lou looks up and groans, "Who let *those* kids in?"

53

"My triplets have something to say," says their Dad.
"We are sorry we hurt your cat. We feel bad."
"We are trying to be ninjas," one rat is explaining.
Lou rolls her eyes. "You need to keep training."

At eight o'clock sharp the Bob Band plays a set.
Ms. Pat and Sal's Gramps perform a duet.
Eddie, who works for Bonefish Street Power
Says his team is fixing the transformer tower.

But this Bonefish Street Bash does not need more light.
Good Neighbor Power makes it a great night.

CHAPTER 10
SORTING CANDY

"We did it!" cries Lou. "Now let's sort our candy.
Those extra large bags sure did come in handy."
"Unwrapped candy gets tossed," cautions Dean.
"That's a Bobs and Tweets rule for a safe Halloween."

"Are you sad, Sal?" asks Dean, "you seem kind of blue.
Did those rat ninja triplets bother you too?"
"No," says Sal, "but I messed up your goal.
We had no treats at my house, no candy bowl."

"Do not worry," says Lou. "We wrote it all down.
That we went to the home of the new kid in town.
And we got the best treat of all, in the end.
A great kid named Sal who is our new friend."